Dear Parent:
Your child's love of reading starts here!

Every child learns to read in a different way and at his or her own speed. Some go back and forth between reading levels and read favorite books again and again. Others read through each level in order. You can help your young reader improve and become more confident by encouraging his or her own interests and abilities. From books your child reads with you to the first books he or she reads alone, there are I Can Read Books for every stage of reading:

SHARED READING
Basic language, word repetition, and whimsical illustrations, ideal for sharing with your emergent reader

BEGINNING READING
Short sentences, familiar words, and simple concepts for children eager to read on their own

READING WITH HELP
Engaging stories, longer sentences, and language play for developing readers

READING ALONE
Complex plots, challenging vocabulary, and high-interest topics for the independent reader

ADVANCED READING
Short paragraphs, chapters, and exciting themes for the perfect bridge to chapter books

I Can Read Books have introduced children to the joy of reading since 1957. Featuring award-winning authors and illustrators and a fabulous cast of beloved characters, I Can Read Books set the standard for beginning readers.

A lifetime of discovery begins with the magical words "I Can Read!"

Visit www.icanread.com for information
on enriching your child's reading experience.

For Peter and Laura,
and their prizewinning pup,
Huckleberry!
—A.S.C.

HarperCollins®, ☛®, and I Can Read Book® are trademarks of HarperCollins Publishers Inc.

Biscuit Wins a Prize Text copyright © 2004 by Alyssa Satin Capucilli Illustrations copyright © 2004 by Pat Schories All rights reserved. No part of this book may be used or reproduced in any manner whatsoever without written permission except in the case of brief quotations embodied in critical articles and reviews. Printed in the United States of America. For information address HarperCollins Children's Books, a division of HarperCollins Publishers, 1350 Avenue of the Americas, New York, NY 10019. www.harperchildrens.com

Library of Congress Cataloging-in-Publication Data
Capucilli, Alyssa Satin
  Biscuit wins a prize / story by Alyssa Satin Capucilli ; pictures by Pat Schories.
    p.   cm. — (My first I can read book)
  Summary: Biscuit, a small puppy, gets excited when he is entered in a pet show.
  ISBN-10: 0-06-009455-9 (trade bdg.) — ISBN-13: 978-0-06-009455-3 (trade bdg.)
  ISBN-10: 0-06-009457-5 (lib. bdg.) — ISBN-13: 978-0-06-009457-7 (lib. bdg.)
  ISBN-10: 0-06-009458-3 (pbk.) — ISBN-13: 978-0-06-009458-4 (pbk.)
  [1. Dogs—Fiction. 2. Pet shows—Fiction.] I. Schories, Pat, ill. II. Title. III. Series.
PZ7.C179Bitc 2004
[E]—dc21
2002154809
CIP
AC

❖

I Can Read!

SHARED My First READING

Biscuit
Wins a Prize

story by ALYSSA SATIN CAPUCILLI
pictures by PAT SCHORIES

HarperCollins*Publishers*

Here, Biscuit.

It's time for the pet show!

Woof, woof!

There will be lots of pets,
and prizes, too!
Woof, woof!

Come along, sweet puppy.

You want to look your best.

Woof!

Hold still, Biscuit.

Woof, woof!

Funny puppy! Don't tug now!

Hold still, Biscuit.

Woof, woof!

Oh, Biscuit!

It's not time to roll over.

Woof, woof!

It's time for the pet show!

Look at all the pets, Biscuit.

Woof, woof!

Biscuit sees his friend Puddles.

Bow wow!

Woof, woof!

Biscuit sees his friend Sam.

Ruff!

Woof, woof!

13

Biscuit sees
lots of new friends, too.

Woof, woof!

Hold still now, Biscuit.

Here comes the judge.

Woof!

Oh no, Biscuit. Come back!

Biscuit wants
to see the fish.
Woof!

Biscuit wants
to see the bunnies.
Woof!

Woof, woof!

Biscuit wants

to see all of the pets

at the pet show!

Silly puppy! Here you are.

What prize will you win now?

Woof, woof!

Oh, Biscuit!

You won the best prize of all!

Woof!